Published by Raintree,
an imprint of Capstone Global Library Limited,
a company incorporated in England and
Wales having its registered office at
264 Banbury Road, Oxford, OX2 7DY –
Registered company number: 6695582

www.raintree.co.uk
myorders@raintree.co.uk

STAR39416

ISBN 978 1 474 75067 7
21 20 19 18 17
10 9 8 7 6 5 4 3 2 1

A full catalogue record for this book is available from
the British Library.

Editor: Christopher Harbo
Designer: Hilary Wacholz

Printed and bound in China.

BATMAN & ROBIN
ADVENTURES

THE RIDDLER'S
BATTLESHIP BLITZ

BY J. E. BRIGHT

ILLUSTRATED BY
TIM LEVINS

COVER ILLUSTRATION BY
LUCIANO VECCHIO

BATMAN CREATED BY BOB KANE
WITH BILL FINGER

CONTENTS

CHAPTER 1

WHICH BRAIN? WHOSE WAR?

"Look, Batman!" said Robin. He leaned forward in the passenger seat of the Batmobile and pointed upwards.

Batman peered up at the purplish dawn sky above Gotham City. Instead of a yellow Bat-Signal, a green question mark beamed against the top of Wayne Tower. It was the city's tallest skyscraper and the headquarters for Wayne Enterprises. "Dr Arkham warned us only ten minutes ago that the Riddler escaped from his cell tonight," he said. "He's already causing trouble."

"Something's weird about the Riddler's signal," noticed Robin. "It's flickering."

Batman put the Batmobile on autopilot as he stared up at the glowing projection. "Hmm," he said. "I recognize those flickers."

"Maybe there's a short-circuit?" Robin guessed.

"No," replied Batman, "it's a pattern. Short and long pulses. It's Morse code. The message is repeating."

"I'm recording it," said Robin. "The Batcomputer can work out what it means."

Batman tapped the side of his head. "I've already translated the code," he said. "It's a riddle, of course. It says '*The war of the world had come again and gone, but its brains were as important as its brawn. What have I stolen to switch on?*'"

"The war of the worlds?" gasped Robin. "Is the Riddler talking about an alien invasion?"

"That's not how I read it," said Batman. "The Riddler wrote *world*, not *worlds*. We've had two major international conflicts called world wars in our history."

The Batmobile rumbled across a bridge into the outskirts of Gotham City. The light was getting brighter as the sun began to rise.

"So which world war is the Riddler riddling us about?" asked Robin.

"'*The war of the world had come again and gone*,'" repeated Batman, thinking about the villain's words. "The Riddler may be referring to World War II."

The Batmobile turned onto the back roads behind Wayne Manor. The entrance to the Batcave was hidden in a thicket of trees.

"World War II was a global war between the Allies and the Axis powers in Europe and Asia," said Robin as they zoomed through the woods. "That much I know. The Axis powers were Germany, Japan and Italy. The Allies were mostly everyone else, including –" Robin ticked the names of the countries off on his gloved fingers. "Britain, France, Poland . . . and eventually the United States, the Soviet Union –" He ended up on his thumb again. "And China."

"Good, Robin," said Batman. "Those are the basic facts. There were a lot of shifting sides in the war, which lasted from 1939 to 1945. It's all extremely complicated. But I'm glad to hear you listened to a little of your history lesson."

"Hey, I listened to all of it," protested Robin. "Remembering is the tricky part."

Batman smiled. "Let's work on the riddle inside," he said. "I'm hungry after our night on patrol. I hope Alfred has breakfast ready."

"Indeed I do," said his butler Alfred over the Batmobile's radio.

The Batmobile blazed towards a cliff wall covered in leafy bushes. The self-driving car didn't slow down. Collision with the cliff seemed impossible to avoid.

CHOOM! At the last moment, a wide trapdoor opened at the base of the cliff. Inside was a ramp heading underground, which the Batmobile roared down smoothly. The trapdoor closed behind them.

It only took a few minutes for the Batmobile to rumble down the tunnel to the main section of the Batcave. The Batmobile parked in a big garage between the Batcycle and Robin's Redbird motorcycle.

After exiting the Batmobile, Robin peered into a scanner on a panel beside a vault door. The scanner analysed his eyeball. The steel door slid aside, letting Batman and Robin into their secret headquarters.

Alfred waited for them on the other side. "Efficient patrol tonight, sirs?" he asked.

"Yes, Alfred," replied Batman. "Mostly petty crimes. One minor rescue of a woman trapped in an elevator."

"Then on the way home we spotted the Riddler's riddle," added Robin.

"Yes, I saw the Morse code recording on the computer link," said Alfred. "A most perplexing brain-teaser. I've set up breakfast by the Batcomputer's central workstation so you can continue solving the puzzle."

"Thank you, Alfred," said Batman.

Alfred bowed and led them to a changing area. There Batman and Robin swapped their uniforms for dressing gowns and slippers. The cavernous Batcave was chilly deep under the ground.

Dressed in these ordinary clothes, Batman and Robin preferred to think of themselves as their true identities, Bruce Wayne and Tim Drake.

Bruce went through another set of steel sliding vault doors into the main cavern of the Batcave. The enormous stone chamber had been carved out by an underground stream over many centuries.

Against the cavern's far wall were souvenirs from Batman and Robin's adventures. The keepsakes included a giant Lincoln penny, a huge joker playing card and a life-size robotic Tyrannosaurus rex.

In the middle of the cavern loomed a huge free-standing media tower covered in monitors. The screens showed Bruce video feeds from around Gotham City and the world beyond.

A ring of control panels around a hi-tech chair made up Batman's command centre. From there he could run his incredibly powerful Batcomputer. On Bruce's right, Tim had his own computer terminal, set up as a long desk with no chairs. Tim preferred to stand so he could be active while interacting with the system.

While Bruce ate breakfast, he called up the riddle on his main screen. It floated in green letters in front of him:

The war of the world had come again and gone, but its brains were as important as its brawn. What have I stolen to switch on?

Bruce had already worked out the first part: that was World War II. But he wasn't sure what the Riddler meant by the second line. "What or whose brains were famous at that time?" he asked.

"Albert Einstein?" guessed Tim.

"He was alive then, but not directly involved in the fighting," said Bruce, tapping his lips. "Perhaps J. Robert Oppenheimer, who helped develop the atomic bomb."

"Kaboom and kablooie, Bruce," said Tim, almost choking on a waffle. "You don't think the Riddler stole a nuclear weapon, do you? If that's what he's going to switch on –"

"Don't panic," said Bruce. "I would have heard if a nuclear device had been stolen. And an atomic bomb isn't the Riddler's style."

"So what's he talking about?" asked Tim.

"Hmm," said Bruce. "Batcomputer, make a list of important brains of World War II."

The Batcomputer beeped. Bruce scrolled through the list of results. He passed by listings for scholars, political thinkers and writers.

Then he read the name Alan Turing.

"Ah," said Bruce.

"Alan Turing?" asked Tim. "Oh, he kind of invented the computer!"

"Turing was a British mathematician," said Bruce.

"A personal hero of mine," said Alfred. "His computer science theories led him to create an electromagnetic thinking machine."

Alfred typed on a keyboard at a workstation, calling up more information.

"Here it is," the butler continued. "He used that machine to decipher supposedly unbreakable messages, known as ciphers, from the Germans during the war. By doing so, Turing helped to end the war and saved millions of lives."

"Interesting," said Bruce. "Alfred, tell Tim the name of the German cipher system."

"I believe the Germans used a device called the Enigma Machine," replied Alfred.

"Yes," said Bruce. "Tim, what is the Riddler's real name?"

"Um . . . Edward Nygma," said Tim. "He used to work at Wayne Enterprises as a scientist himself, back before he went bonkers."

"E. Nygma," Bruce pointed out. "Too close to Enigma be a coincidence, I think."

"Wow," said Tim. "So you think the Riddler stole an Enigma Machine?"

"Maybe," answered Bruce. "We do have one in Gotham City. It's on the old battleship USS *New Jersey*. The ship was turned into a military museum in the harbour."

"I'm looking up the USS *New Jersey* museum now," said Tim. "Maybe their website has more info about the Enigma Machine."

After pulling up the Gotham Military Museum's home page, Tim clicked on World War II. "Look, they have a section about codes and ciphers," he said. He clicked on the link for ENIGMA MACHINE.

Suddenly, the Batcomputer beeped in alarm. Then all the monitors went black, blinked and the giggling face of the Riddler appeared on all of the screens.

HA! HA! HA! HA! HA!

The sound of laughter echoed through the Batcave. The Riddler tapped his green bowler hat. "You worked out the first part with aplomb," he said. "But when is a bomb not a bomb? You'll find no calm at this dot-com!"

The crazy villain broke out in laughter again as his image fuzzed. The monitors crackled as the screens flickered wildly. The displays flashed faster, sizzling with sparks.

The monitors went black as smoke poured out of their back panels.

WHOOSH!

All the screens burst into flames.

CHAPTER 2

CODES AND CIPHERS

Alfred strode over to a red cabinet. He pulled out a fire extinguisher and passed it to Tim. "Spray the monitors," he said.

Tim hit the nozzle and thick foam gushed out onto the media tower. *FFSSSSHH!*

The fires fizzled out, leaving a mess of melted plastic.

"Was our system hacked?" asked Tim. "Does the Riddler know where we are?"

"No, I don't think so," said Bruce. "The Riddler knew we would check that website. He must have hidden an overload command in the code. Alfred, make an anonymous call to the museum and tell them that Batman and Robin are on their way."

"Perhaps you should rest first," said Alfred. "You were out all night on patrol."

"Yes, that's best," replied Bruce. "We're going to need our wits about us to beat the Riddler at whatever sneaky game he's playing this time. Tell the museum we'll be there this afternoon."

* * *

By the time Batman and Robin arrived at the harbour, the sky was darkening. Batman parked the Batmobile on the pier beside the battleship.

The USS *New Jersey* was a massive grey vessel the length of three football pitches. It bristled with communication antennae, gun turrets and missile launchers. Three different helicopters sat on its wide deck, along with a vintage propeller aeroplane and a sleek modern jet.

A smartly dressed woman with a tight blonde ponytail met the Dynamic Duo at the main entrance. "Batman, thank you for coming," she said. "Hello, Robin. I'm Henrietta Lebam, director of the Gotham City Military Museum." She ushered them inside the ship. "How did you hear about the stolen historical equipment? We haven't reported the theft to the police yet."

"The Riddler sent us clues," Batman answered. "We think he stole an Enigma cipher machine."

"That's who took it," said Director Lebam. She stood with the bearing of a retired military woman, her shoulders back. "I knew only a master criminal could get through our security without triggering any alarms."

"So he did steal your Enigma Machine?" asked Robin.

"Not only that," replied Lebam. She gestured for Batman and Robin to follow her. The director led them deeper into the museum. They passed through rooms showing a range of weapons, naval equipment and military uniforms.

"Watch your step," warned Lebam, as they crossed through an opened bulkhead door. The doorway was oval, with a thick, raised curve on the bottom to help seal the door with its lock wheel in case the ship flooded.

They entered a large room dedicated to military intelligence, decorated with posters and display cases. Batman and Robin walked past glass cases featuring spy equipment. They saw a shoe with a hidden compartment, a key ring fob that was a camera and a wallet with a switchblade-style knife.

Past the spycraft area, a section of the wall had the words CODES AND CIPHERS printed on it. Against the wall stood a giant glass case. Next to it was a smaller case on a pedestal. Both were empty.

"See?" asked Lebam, peering into the big, glass box. "He also stole a machine that was built to decipher the Enigma's messages."

"The American Bombe," Robin read from the sign on the empty case. "Am I pronouncing that right . . . just like *bomb*?"

"Yes," said Director Lebam. "During World War II, Polish code breakers developed a device they called the bomba. Its name came from the whirring sound it made – like it was about to explode. Alan Turning in England built his version of the bombe to decipher secret messages the Germans made using their Enigma Machine."

"And that bombe broke the German codes?" asked Robin.

"Ciphers, not codes," said Lebam. "Although the difference is not always clear, and usually it comes down to shades of meaning."

"Codes often change words or phrases for convenience – such as simplifying a code for communication," Batman said. "Ciphers are used to hide information. Codes are not always meant to be secret."

"Oh," said Robin. "That's why anyone can learn Morse code."

"Correct," said Lebam. "Morse code turned the alphabet into dots and dashes to simplify communication for telegraph machine operators. The Germans' Enigma Machine turned messages into encrypted ciphers that the bombes were built to unravel."

"Hmm," said Batman. "That last riddle the Riddler sent us: *'when is a bomb not a bomb?'* This makes sense now. The answer is . . . when it's a *bombe*."

"Yes," agreed Lebam. "All the British bombes were destroyed after the war to help keep their existence a secret. But the British shared their intelligence with US engineers. In 1944, the US Navy built the bombe that sat here so that we could decipher the Germans' messages too."

"So what does the Riddler want with these machines?" asked Robin. "Is there some code somewhere he needs to break? I mean, some cipher he needs to . . . decipher?"

"Good question," said Lebam. "The bombe was designed specifically to crack the Enigma's ciphers. While it could be used to work out other ciphers, any modern computer works much faster."

Robin peered into the oversized glass display case where the bombe was kept. "And computers are much smaller."

"Oh, yes," said Lebam. "See the picture of the bombe on the information sign? It was the size of several five-drawer filing cabinets. It had wires all over it and several rotors and dials. It's a mystery how the Riddler got the bombe out of the case without breaking it. Or how he got it out of the museum."

"The Riddler loves giving us mysteries to solve," said Batman. "If you don't mind, we'll start by investigating in this area."

"Be my guest," said Director Lebam, stepping out of the way.

Batman started with the smaller display case, bending down to inspect it. Its pedestal had a sign reading GERMAN ENIGMA MACHINE c.1942. From the picture on the information sign, the machine looked like an antique typewriter connected to a wooden box of gear-wheel dials.

The glass of the display case was clean. "No fingerprints," Batman said. "But the Riddler always wears gloves."

"The glass box is fused to the pedestal," said Lebam. "He would have had to cut the glass, but that would leave a mark. Or an empty pane."

"Perhaps it did," replied Batman. He crouched down beside the pedestal. The glass box was lit from above by a spotlight, now hitting the empty space where the Enigma Machine had been. "Director, would you please turn off that light?"

"The controls are on a main panel in a central room," said Lebam. "I'll be right back." She strode out of the spycraft area.

Batman took a compact device that was both a microscope and telescope out of his Utility Belt. "Robin," he said, "give me your torch, please."

Robin handed Batman his little torch just as the spotlights in the ceiling turned off.

Batman held the lens of the microscope up to his eye. He bent closer to the glass case as he adjusted the microscope to increase the magnification.

Then he shined Robin's torch into the side of the glass pane from below.

Batman smiled. "There's a hairline shadow along the base," said Batman. "This is impressive glass cutting. And repair. It must have been cut by diamond, so finely that the seam disappears in the bright overhead spotlight. The cut is in a strange pattern . . ."

Standing up, Batman nodded to Director Lebam as she hurried back into the compartment. Then he put his gloved hands on either side of the glass box. Instead of lifting it, he pulled gently. The case slid slowly towards him. It had been cut in an interlocking pattern and refitted back together like a glass puzzle.

"That's a Greek key pattern," noticed Lebam. "Also known as a meander."

"Wow," said Robin. "Really, he could have just smashed the glass."

"That's not who the Riddler is," replied Batman. "We have to think like him to capture him."

"Okay," said Robin, spinning his eyes in a crazy expression. "I'm thinking like the Riddler."

Robin turned towards the big glass box that had held the American Bombe. "How can I make opening this case overcomplicated and annoying?" he said. "Let's see if it slides."

Robin put his gloved hands on the side of the empty bombe case.

"Wait," said Batman as Robin pushed the glass.

CRICK! CRACKLE! POOF!

The whole box disintegrated into dust. What had looked like a big rectangle of floor under the display crumbled too, leaving a gaping hole.

Caught off balance, Robin windmilled his arms, his boots teetering on the edge. Below him was a serious drop to a lower deck far below.

Lebam jumped forwards, trying to grab Robin's cape. But the Boy Wonder, with his acrobatic reflexes, caught himself and stepped back – and Lebam missed.

The museum director tumbled head first into the hole.

CHAPTER 3

YOU ALMOST SANK MY BATTLESHIP

Robin fell flat on his stomach against the floor. He jammed out his hand, clasping his grip around Lebam's arm. He gritted his teeth as the director's weight jarred his shoulder. Beyond Lebam's dangling feet, the American Bombe sat directly underneath on the floor far below.

"Here, pull her up," said Batman, helping Lebam back to safety while peering over the edge. "Something's wrong with the floor down there. Around the device there's another seam."

All three looked down as a final piece of debris fell onto the bombe. The device whirred loudly as if it was going to explode. But instead of bursting into flames, the rectangle of floor around it gave way. It fell through the bottom of the battleship.

"It was a booby trap," said Robin.

"Oh no!" Lebam cried, as the American Bombe sank into the harbour below the ship.

GURGLE! GURGLE! Greyish-green gushes of water burbled up from the rectangular hole. The water spouted into the ship, flooding the steel floor.

"Get Lebam out of this room," Batman ordered Robin. "The water will reach up here too. Lock the bulkhead door behind you."

Then Batman jumped down into the fountain of water below. *SPLOOSH!*

The spouting water cushioned his fall, and he slid into the rising flood in the lower storage room. Storage boxes and stacks of folding tables and chairs floated around him.

The winter ocean was frigid. Batman's uniform protected him from the worst of the chill, but he still felt the cold like icy knives. He dodged a floating folding table and waded across the storage room.

Past the hole in the floor, Batman let the water push him towards the open bulkhead door on the other side. He bobbed towards the raised lip on the doorway and tumbled into the metal corridor past it.

Batman struggled to his feet, fighting the painfully cold water. He grabbed the edge of the bulkhead door and slid himself behind it. From there he shoved his feet against the wall and his back against the door.

Batman forced the hatch towards the doorway against the push of the water. If he didn't get it closed immediately, the battleship would sink – with Director Lebam, Robin and all its military treasures.

Just before the door closed, a folding chair got wedged between it and the wall. It blocked Batman from pushing the door closed completely. The water kept gushing in through the small opening.

Batman stood propped up against the wall. He couldn't stop pushing the door or it would pop open again. He narrowed his eyes, struggling to hold the door shut. How would he get the chair out of the doorway?

The water level in the corridor continued to rise. It reached Batman's outstretched legs, causing them to shiver. He wasn't sure how much longer he could keep pushing the door.

Gritting his teeth, Batman shut his eyes to focus on holding the bulkhead door as closed as he could.

"Batman!" called Robin.

Batman glanced up to see his partner sloshing his way down the corridor.

"Pull out that chair, Robin," Batman instructed. "But brace yourself for a hard hit of water."

Robin grabbed the chair and got a good grip on its metal legs.

Batman bent his knees, releasing the door a little.

With a yank, Robin pulled out the folding chair. He let go. Pushed by the rush of water, the chair clattered down the corridor behind him. Then Robin thrust his shoulder against the hatch, helping Batman to close the door.

CLANG! The door slammed shut. Batman spun the hatch's wheel, keeping the ocean locked out on the other side.

"The Riddler is insane," Robin gasped. "He tried to sink the battleship."

"He didn't succeed," said Batman. "How is Director Lebam?"

"Thanks to Robin, I'm shipshape," called Lebam as she approached through the puddles of the draining water. "Which is more than I can say about my museum. I'm grateful you stopped the flooding before the ship went down. I understand why the Riddler would want to steal the Enigma Machine, but why sink the battleship?"

"The Riddler always has his reasons," said Batman. "He can't resist leaving a riddle behind to explain his crimes . . . and to give us a clue to the next one."

"Maybe there's another riddle hidden on the ship," suggested Robin.

"It stands to reason," said Batman. "Let's find it. Contact me if you find anything unusual, but don't touch anything until I'm there."

Batman, Robin and Director Lebam split up to search the USS *New Jersey*. Robin headed to the bridge, where the battleship's steering, navigation and communication controls were located. Lebam searched the mess hall and barracks where sailors lived while they were at sea. After Batman cruised through the gift shop, he climbed stairs to the upper deck to look over the aeroplanes and helicopters.

Outside, the air was chilly and breezy. Batman's cape flapped behind him as he walked over to the aeroplanes.

He passed a seaplane used to sink submarines and walked alongside a small dive-bomber that destroyed enemy ships during World War II. But Batman couldn't see any sign of a message from the Riddler.

Nearby were several military helicopters from World War II, the Korean War and the Vietnam War. Beside them, in a space protected from the wind, a single balloon bobbed on a string. It was attached to the railings of the battleship.

Batman approached the balloon warily. "Robin," he radioed his partner, "come in. I found something unusual on the helicopter pad. Bring Lebam up here too."

The wind shifted and the balloon bounced gently, turning sideways. Batman could see that it was an oval shape, like a rugby ball or a blimp.

Batman waited at a distance for Robin and Lebam to arrive. He saw tiny writing on the balloon. It was probably another riddle, but he hadn't got close enough to read it yet.

Robin and Director Lebam hurried past the planes towards him.

"I didn't want to touch it until you were here," said Batman. "Or even get any closer. That way we can protect each other in case it explodes or springs some other nasty trick. Warn me if anything looks suspicious at any point, all right?"

"You got it," said Robin. "Be careful."

"Good luck," said Lebam.

Stepping carefully, Batman creeped towards the balloon. He held his breath so that he wouldn't accidentally trigger some kind of trap.

After a few more steps, Batman got close enough to make out the writing on its side. He read aloud:

"Bombe's away, is what I say! Your device has sunk to the deep. But don't be a wimp, take a ride on my blimp, a ticket for this riddle's quite cheap. Don't get irritable on the terrible dirigible, it's an airship equipped for a one-way trip. Just board my zeppelin to take your medicine, then mutter your name in your sleep."

The second Batman stopped speaking, the balloon burst with a loud *POP!*

Batman braced himself for a fiery blast, or toxic gas, but the balloon just fell – flat and limp – to the steel deck. Nothing else happened.

Robin laughed. "What a dud!" he said. "I was scared there for a second."

"The Riddler does keep us on our toes," admitted Batman. He bent over and picked up a tattered piece of the popped balloon. "The message concerns me, though."

"It seems pretty straightforward," said Robin. "He's going to attack a blimp, and we need to stop him."

"That's what worries me," replied Batman. "It's too straightforward. Most of it isn't really a riddle. And which blimp is he talking about? Lots of advertising blimps circle Gotham City every day."

Director Lebam pointed out across the dark expanse of Gotham Harbour. "Look over there," she said. "There's a new sightseeing blimp tour that started this week. See the flashing lights of its LED display over the marina? Maybe that's the blimp the Riddler meant."

"It's our only clue to what the Riddler will do next," said Batman. He looked at Robin. "It looks like we're going on a blimp tour."

"I'll need to prepare the *New Jersey's* engines to pilot it to the shipyard for repairs," said Lebam. "Good luck catching the Riddler. He deserves a lifetime in prison for sinking the rare and irreplaceable American Bombe."

"We'll make sure justice is served," replied Batman. "Come on, Robin. Let's go and catch a blimp."

"And hopefully a thief," replied the Boy Wonder.

CHAPTER 4

BLIMP BLUNDER

Just over twenty minutes later, Batman and Robin stood on the observation deck of a gondola hanging from the underside of a huge blimp. It slowly cruised above the commercial area of Gotham City.

"What a classy way to travel," said Robin, "and the ride is so smooth."

"Like floating on air?" Batman teased.

A couple of older tourists laughed at Batman's joke. But other passengers seemed nervous to have the Dynamic Duo on board.

Batman didn't blame them. Their arrival often meant a dangerous crime was in progress. But he and Robin were there to keep them safe. They had to stay alert for any sign of the Riddler's fiendish plan.

"How will I mutter my name in my sleep?" he asked Robin in a whisper. "Why is this airship only equipped for a one-way trip? And what medicine is on the zeppelin?"

"I'm keeping a lookout for anything unusual," said Robin.

Batman scanned the area. The gondola under the blimp was a long, capsule-shaped room with floor-to-ceiling windows all along its curved walls. Padded benches gave passengers plenty of comfortable space to sit and enjoy the view. There was a snack bar at the back. A locked security door at the front of the ship led to the cockpit.

About twenty-five tourists, including ten children, stared out of the windows, pointing out the city's attractions from above. Everyone oohed and ahhed about the expanse of Robinson Park, the dome of STAR Labs, and the tall skyscraper of Wayne Tower. A large TV screen by the snack bar showed images of locations below.

Suddenly the gondola lurched. Batman grabbed the back of a bench to steady himself. A small girl grabbed his hand to keep from falling.

"What's happening?" the girl wailed.

"I'd like to know that too," said Batman.

The blimp started to sink.

"This got bad fast," said Robin.

On the big TV screen, a picture of the Riddler's grinning face popped up.

"And just got worse," said Batman.

"Hello, kiddies, old folks, tourists and the Dynamic Duo," the Riddler said on-screen. "Thank you for flying Riddler Airways. We're going to land faster than you had planned, but first I've got a riddle for you."

These words flashed on the screen while the Riddler read them aloud:

"I affect all creatures for hours each day, I show you strange visions while you are away, but sometimes don't stop what you're dying to say. I work best when you're safe in your bed, with your secrets and fears playing in your head. Sometimes I'm mistaken for mimicking the dead."

"I think I know," said Robin.

"Sleep," said the little girl holding onto Batman's hand.

"That's what I was going to say," Robin protested. Then he opened his mouth wide in a huge yawn. "Oh, excuse me. Is it weird that I feel like saying my real name –"

"Robin," Batman ordered sternly, "put your gas mask on now."

Robin did as he was told, and Batman did the same. As they covered their faces, Batman spotted a tiny leak in the ceiling of the gondola. *HISSS!* A thick, greenish fog clouded the room.

The tourists yawned too. They lay down on the benches, and some just slumped to the floor in sleep.

Batman gently helped the girl onto a bench. She curled up and started snoring.

"Sally's a better friend than Molly," the little girl muttered. "There, I said it."

An old man sleeping on a bench shifted uncomfortably. "The money's in the mattress," he whispered. "Don't tell anyone."

"The secret ingredient is nutmeg," admitted a sleeping woman nearby.

"It's some kind of sleeping truth gas," said Robin, his voice muffled by his mask.

"No doubt meant for us," replied Batman. "Hmm. The Riddler said we would mutter our names in our sleep. That's it. He's trying to find out our true identities."

"A riddle he can't resist," said Robin.

"I ate all the strawberries," a young boy moaned.

All around, the tourists were telling their secrets in their sleep. Meanwhile, the blimp was sinking faster as the sleeping truth gas escaped the balloon.

"Oh, drat," said the Riddler from the TV screen. "I was worried you had masks. No matter, the blimp was just a distraction. Look at the USS *New Jersey* to catch the action."

Batman and Robin rushed over to the nearest window. In the harbour, the battleship was pulling away from the wharf. Tiny figures hopped angrily on the dock. Through his telescope, Batman saw Lebam shaking her fist at the stolen battleship.

"Thank you for getting the museum to turn on its engines for me," said the Riddler.

"Put that battleship back, Riddler," said Batman. "You know we'll stop you."

"Did I say I could hear you up there, Batman?" asked the Riddler. "No. But if you survive this crash, you'll tell me your identity soon enough. Now have fun – this landing will be rough!"

The screen fizzled and went black.

"We're sinking faster," Robin warned.

"We need to land this blimp now," said Batman. Jumping over sleeping people, he ran over to the cockpit door. It was locked, so he put his ear to the metal door to listen.

"I don't even like blimps," Batman heard a pilot say in his sleep on the other side. "I wanted to be an astronaut."

"I still live with my parents," the other pilot admitted.

Batman took his lock picks out of his Utility Belt. He inserted a pick into the lock and gently turned it. The door swung open.

Batman and Robin rushed into the cockpit. The view was tilted at an alarming downward angle, with the harbour closer and larger than Batman expected.

They pulled the pilots out of their seats and laid them on the floor. Then they strapped themselves into the seats. Batman grabbed the controls.

He quickly levelled out the blimp, but he could do nothing to stop it from dropping. The blimp had lost too much gas, which was still trickling out. Batman estimated that he could land the airship before they crashed. But where he landed would make a big difference.

He scanned the harbour for suitable places. A water landing might be softest, but he also didn't want to drown all the sleeping passengers. So that was out. He considered aiming for the trees in the Gotham City Botanical Gardens, but that would destroy many of the rare plants.

"Where can we land?" asked Robin.

"I've got an idea," replied Batman through his mask.

The Dark Knight adjusted the direction of the airship with the metal pedals on the floor. He steered the blimp towards the USS *New Jersey* pulling out into the open harbour.

The blimp's control systems were rather old-fashioned. There was no computer landing procedure. Batman would have to land the blimp by hand.

Speeding up as it lost air, the blimp dropped towards the battleship. Batman struggled to hold the airship level so that it didn't fall too fast.

"Hold on," he said to Robin. "We're coming in hot."

"If only we could cushion our fall," Robin said, gripping the armrests of his seat.

"Hmm," said Batman. "That gives me another idea."

Instead of levelling out the blimp, he aimed the airship straight downwards. It picked up speed. He pushed the throttle, urging the engines to make the blimp fly even faster.

"Bad idea!" cried Robin.

"Trust me," said Batman.

The battleship loomed bigger as they plummeted towards it, until its central tower filled their whole view. They were heading straight for the battleship's control bridge, a box-like command centre with a row of narrow windows around its middle.

Moments before they crashed, Batman pulled back on the throttle. The blimp slowed down as it veered towards the flat wall under the bridge tower, balloon first.

With a teeth-jarring thump, the blimp bumped into the bridge. *BONK!* Acting like a massive airbag, the balloon bounced the blimp off the tower.

Both Batman and Robin lurched forward from the force of the impact. Robin bit his lip in the collision, but their seat belts saved them from worse injury.

Righting itself in the air, the airship dropped down, smacking the flat base of the gondola against the battleship's metal deck. Batman felt the thump in his bones, but they had slowed down enough that the gondola's carbon-fibre frame absorbed the fall.

The blimp banged against the deck a few more times before coming to a scraping, screeching stop.

"The Riddler was right," groaned Robin. "That was rough."

"But we're alive," said Batman. He felt
the pilots' necks for a pulse. "They're unhurt.
Just sleeping. Come on, let's check on the
passengers."

They rushed back into the gondola's main
compartment. Nobody seemed injured other
than some scrapes and bruises. Relaxed in
slumber, the tourists had survived the crash-
landing safely.

"Let's let them dream for now," said
Batman through his mask. "They're better
off missing what comes next."

"The Riddler's going to put up a fight,"
agreed Robin.

"Yes," said Batman. "There's going to be a
battle on this battleship."

CHAPTER 5

THE BATTLESHIP'S MINE

With simultaneous kicks, Batman and
Robin banged open the gondola's exit hatch.
They shut the door behind them so that the
remaining gas didn't escape.

Once they were safe on the deck, they
removed their gas masks. Batman readied
his Batarangs and Robin extended his
telescoping bo staff, both on high alert. They
had no element of surprise on their side. The
Riddler couldn't have missed their arrival in
a crashing blimp.

But as they approached the upper deck's entrance, the villain was nowhere to be seen. The only sound was the splashing of water against the metal ship's hull.

"Strange," said Batman. "The Riddler has turned the ship around. We're heading back towards the dock."

Batman peered up at the control bridge in the tower, but he couldn't see the Riddler through the glass. Still, he assumed that's where the villain would make his base of operations. Up close, the tower looked as strong as a fortress.

Robin grabbed the handle of the armoured door at the base of the tower.

"Wait," said Batman. He gestured for Robin to stand alongside the door, not in front of it. Batman stood on the other side. He reached over and opened the door.

VOOOSH! A small missile blasted out, trailing fire. It soared into the harbour, splashed down and exploded. *CHOOM!*

Batman peeked around the edge of the door. The Riddler was standing inside, laughing, with a missile launcher from the museum's collection.

"I missed the first one," said the Riddler. "But the fun's just begun! This battleship is fully operational. The destruction it can cause is sensational! All the ship's rockets are aimed at Wayne Tower . . . tell me your real names, or I'll show you their power."

The Riddler laughed again and ran down the corridor. He hurtled up a set of stairs to the bridge, locking the door behind him.

"What can we do, Batman?" Robin asked. "There are thousands of people in Wayne Tower. We can't risk attacking him."

Batman narrowed his eyes. "We've got to cut power to the bridge," he said, "and take away his control of the rockets." He pinged his butler on his mask communicator. "Alfred, go down to the Batcave, please."

"I'm already here, sir," said Alfred. "Tidying up. I have finished replacing the melted computer monitors."

"Thank you," said Batman. "Please call up blueprints for the battleship USS *New Jersey*. I need to know how to cut power to the main bridge controls."

"Yes, sir," said Alfred. "One moment, please."

"I believe the power controls are on the second level," said Batman, gesturing for Robin to follow him downstairs. "That's where Director Lebam went to turn off the lights in the museum."

Batman and Robin hurried down a few twisting corridors through the battleship. They passed the closed bulkhead door that protected the ship from the flooded spycraft room. There didn't seem to be any leaks.

Down another corridor, Batman found a door labelled ELECTRICAL. It was locked and needed an electronic key card to be opened.

"I don't have time for this," said Batman. He sprang forward and kicked the door right near the lock. It broke open with a clang.

Batman entered and inspected the wall of wires, switches and fuse boxes inside.

Staying out in the corridor, Robin kept lookout.

"Alfred, any information?" asked Batman. "I'm a pretty good electrician, but this system is extremely complex."

"Yes, sir," said Alfred. "I have it. The controls to the rocket launchers should be on the wall's lower north-west corner. Unfortunately, other bridge systems are not housed in your location. Nothing in there will affect navigation, communication and other, older weapons systems."

"Understood," said Batman. "At least we can save the city."

Batman found the box for the missile system. He removed the cover and stared down at the mess of complicated wires. "I'm not feeling subtle," he snarled. Batman grabbed a fist full of wires and yanked them out of the box in a shower of sparks. *SIZZLE!* "That should fix it."

"Yoo-hoo, Batman!" called the Riddler from the corridor. "I get bigger when I eat, but weaker when I drink. What am I?"

"Uh-oh," said Batman. "We've got to get out of here."

He and Robin ran into the corridor and stopped short.

The Riddler stood down the corridor with a device strapped to his back. Over his shoulder was a hose that fed a long, skinny nozzle that he pointed towards the Dynamic Duo.

"You got it!" cheered the Riddler. "Fire!"

He pulled the trigger and a jet of orange flame spouted out of the nozzle in a stream of igniting fuel. *WHOOSH!*

"Flame-thrower!" yelled Robin. "Run!"

Batman and Robin raced down the corridor in the other direction. The Riddler sprinted after them, stopping at every turn into a new corridor to blast another stream of fire at the Dynamic Duo.

After another sharp turn, Batman stopped short a step past the closed door to the storage room. "Robin," he said. "Here."

The heroes stood beside the door, waiting for the Riddler to round the corner.

The Riddler seemed puzzled for a second to find Batman and Robin waiting for him, but then he smiled. "We don't need these games," he said. "Just admit your real names. If I think you are a liar, I'll roast you in an open fire." He aimed the nozzle of the flame-thrower right at Batman.

"Forget it, Riddler," said Batman. "You'll just have to live with the mystery."

"Then it's time for you to fry," replied the Riddler. "Good luck and goodbye."

He pulled the flame-thrower's trigger, shooting out a trail of fire. *WHOOSH!*

"Now!" said Batman. He and Robin grabbed the locking wheel of the storage room's door and spun it. They yanked open the hatch. *GUSSSHHH!*

Churning cold water surged out of the flooded room. Batman and Robin braced themselves against the door, forcing the water towards the Riddler. It flowed down the corridor, flushing the Riddler backwards.

AHHHGH!

The Riddler screamed as he tumbled but fell silent when his head thumped against the back wall of the corridor.

Batman and Robin grunted as they pushed the hatch closed again.

The water drained out of the corridor. They hurried over to the Riddler, who was slumped in the corner, unconscious.

"Out cold," said Robin.

"There's a way to make him talk," said Batman.

Batman grabbed the Riddler and hoisted him onto his shoulder. He carried the villain up to the deck outside.

Robin opened the gondola door of the semi-deflated blimp. Batman dumped the Riddler on the floor. Both Batman and Robin put on gas masks again.

While Robin tied up the Riddler, he and Batman waited for the gas to take effect.

The Riddler twitched. "PUCU ZRTB VYBA HCZE," he muttered.

"What is that nonsense?" asked Robin.

"It's a cipher," said Batman. "From the Enigma Machine. Record it and send a copy to Alfred immediately."

"JJDZ YAZW XYDH PRTH," the Riddler continued to moan unconsciously. "KWBV ERMS DNAI DZEC OMZF! JREP OOOI RMBL XEPV. QOAF SAOC MPIQ EJTM EGYP QZPC. VIBA PTAB OSLR PJKL!"

"Alfred," Batman radioed his butler. "Have you received the cipher?"

"Yes, sir," replied Alfred. "But won't we need the bombe to decipher it?"

"Run it through the Batcomputer," Batman replied. "Director Lebam said computers today are much more powerful than the bombe. The Batcomputer should be able to handle it."

"One moment please, sir," said Alfred.

"Batman, look!" cried Robin. He pointed at a dark shape in the water in front of the moving battleship.

Batman pulled out his compact telescope and peered at the object floating ahead of the battleship. He gritted his teeth as he recognized the giant metal ball bristling with pointy triggers.

"It's a naval mine," Batman groaned. "The Riddler dropped it behind the ship. Then turned us around to head towards it."

"Let's get up to the bridge and drop anchor before we hit it!" said Robin.

They left the Riddler sleeping in the blimp with the tourists and raced up through the tower to the control room of the USS *New Jersey*. Batman rushed to the navigation control computer.

But the screen showed the words: ENTER PASSWORD.

Batman entered ENIGMA.

PASSWORD INCORRECT, the computer screen flashed. ONE MORE ATTEMPT ALLOWED BEFORE SYSTEM SHUTDOWN.

"Okay, I'm not guessing again," said Batman.

"Do you think the answer is in the Riddler's cipher?" asked Robin.

"Let's hope," said Batman. "We're going to hit that mine in three minutes. Alfred, any progress on solving that cipher?"

"I think I have it, sir," said Alfred. "It seems to be another riddle, of course."

"Read it back, Alfred," said Batman.

Alfred read: *"Everything is going fine until Batman blows up with a mine. The only way to enter my secret password is to know who told the riddle Oedipus heard."*

"Oedipus?" cried Robin. "Who's that? We're doomed!"

"Relax, Robin," ordered Batman. "Oedipus was a king in Ancient Greek mythology."

"So what's his riddle?" asked Robin.

"*What goes on four legs in the morning, two legs at noon and three legs in the evening?*" recited Alfred.

"I have no clue," said Robin.

"The answer is *man*," said Batman. "He crawls as a baby, walks upright in the middle of life and uses a cane in old age. It's called the Riddle of the Sphinx, because a giant cat woman told it to him in the myth."

Batman typed SPHINX into the computer.

DING! The battleship's system accepted the password and granted access.

"That mine is too close," said Robin, peering through the bridge's wrap-around windows.

Batman quickly found the computer command that dropped the anchor. He initiated it and was happy to hear chains clanking and a splash as the anchor fell into the harbour.

"Were we fast enough?" Robin asked nervously. "Will the ship stop?"

Centimetres away from the giant naval mine, the USS *New Jersey* lurched to a halt.

"We're safe," said Batman. "Now let's get the tourists back to land and the Riddler back to his cell in Arkham Asylum."

"Absolutely," replied Robin. "I've had enough enigmas – and E. Nygmas – to last a lifetime."

THE RIDDLER

REAL NAME: Edward Nygma

OCCUPATION: Professional criminal

BASE: Gotham City

HEIGHT: 1.8 metres
[6 feet 1 inch]

WEIGHT: 83 kilograms
[183 pounds]

EYES: Blue

HAIR: Black

Even as a little boy, Edward Nygma loved riddles and puzzles. When he grew up, Nygma turned his passion into a career. He became a video game designer and soon invented a popular game called Riddle of the Minotaur. The game sold millions of copies, but Nygma didn't receive a penny from the manufacturer. To get his revenge, Nygma became the Riddler, a cryptic criminal who leaves clues to his crimes.

- The Riddler's cane is shaped like a question mark. This weapon can deliver a shocking blast – the Riddler's answer to his toughest problems.

- The Riddler doesn't just want to break the law. He wants to outsmart Batman as well. Before every crime, the Riddler first sends a clue to Batman.

- The Riddler's real name suits him perfectly. Edward Nygma, or E. Nygma for short, sounds like the word "enigma," which means a mysterious person.

- Harry Houdini is one of the Riddler's greatest heroes. This real-life magician is famous for his stunts, tricks and great escapes.

BIOGRAPHIES

J. E. Bright is the author of many novels, novelizations and novelty books for children and young adults. He lives in Houston, Texas, USA, with his difficult but soft cat, Mabel, and his happy puppy, Henry. Find out more about J. E. Bright on his website.

Tim Levins is best known for his work on the Eisner Award-winning DC Comics series Batman: Gotham Adventures. Tim has illustrated other DC titles, such as Justice League Adventures, Batgirl, Metal Men and Scooby Doo, and has also done work for Marvel Comics and Archie Comics. Tim enjoys life in Midland, Ontario, Canada, with his wife, son and two dogs.

GLOSSARY

anonymous written, done or given by a person whose name is not known or made public

autopilot system that automatically controls a vehicle or weapon

bulkhead wall that separates areas inside a ship

cipher code that uses letters or symbols to represent letters of the alphabet

decipher work out something that is written in code or is hard to understand

dirigible large oval-shaped airship, or zeppelin, with a rigid frame

electromagnetic relating to the combination of electric currents and magnetic fields

encrypt change into a cipher or a code

gondola compartment underneath a hot-air balloon or an airship

vintage from the past

zeppelin large oval-shaped airship, or dirigible, with a rigid frame

DISCUSSION QUESTIONS

1. Why did the Riddler steal the World War II era Enigma Machine? Do you think he planned to use it for a future crime or did he want to have it because his real name is E. Nygma? Explain your answers.

2. The Riddler uses the truth gas on the blimp to trick Batman and Robin into revealing their real names. Why is knowing their real names so important to the Riddler? What do you think would happen if he learned them? Discuss your answers.

3. Most of this story takes place on a floating battleship museum. What is the most interesting museum you have ever visited? Discuss what made it different from other museums.

WRITING PROMPTS

1. Batman and Robin must unravel the Riddler's puzzles to solve his crimes. Write a riddle that gives clues to the location of an object in your home. Then give the riddle to a friend. See if your friend can unravel the clues in your riddle to find the object.

2. History is an important part of this Batman and Robin adventure. Write your own short story adventure that uses an object or event from the past as a main part of the plot.

3. At the end of the story, Batman and Robin plan to take the Riddler to Arkham Asylum. But what if the Riddler escapes from the blimp's gondola before they get there? Write a story that continues the adventure. Where does the Riddler go and how do Batman and Robin finally track him down?

DC

BATMAN & ROBIN
ADVENTURES